ns and plantations,   and mangrove swamps,   to the beach and undersea world

The Rainforest Children

A story set in tropical Australia
By Margaret Pittaway

Illustrated by Heather Philpott

Melbourne
OXFORD UNIVERSITY PRESS
Oxford Wellington New York

for Philippa and Myfanwy

THE QUEENSLAND RAINFOREST

AUSTRALIA

In the north of Australia is a lush, green world, where the air is as damp as air can be, where tall trees crowd together, and where it always seems to be raining.

And there, in the shade of the soft tree-ferns, lived the rainforest children, Rufous and Lantana.

They were small and unafraid, and their bush clothes blended with the colours of the roots and the rocks.

Their friends were the creatures of the day-time and the night-time. Curtains of glossy leaves hid them from the sun. Tangles of vines kept out the wind.

The rainforest children knew the feel of the mossy floor between their toes.

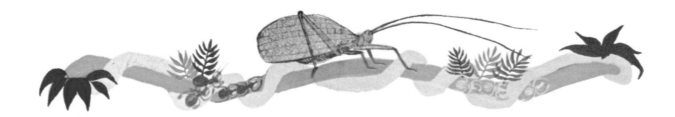

In the early morning gloom, they hardly made a sound as they scurried through the undergrowth.

Lantana often turned the leaf litter to help the birds find earthworms.

Rufous gathered freshly fallen twigs for the ground insects to chew up and add to the soil.

By mid-day, shafts of light dappled the
rotting logs. The lush, green world was noisy
with the sounds of nest-building and feeding.

The rainforest children ate sticky seeds
trapped in the baskets of ferns.

In the quiet afternoon, while even the frogs
slept, Rufous and Lantana played in the forest.
They climbed the woody ropes. They chased
the tree-creepers. And they crept up behind the
rainforest dragons, whose ways and habits
they knew.

At the end of each day, Rufous and Lantana curled up on the fronds of the soft tree-ferns.

The frogs began their night-time chorus, ringtail possums foraged for food, and the gentle mists went drip, drip, drip.

The rainforest children rested.

But one night, Rufous and Lantana heard bushwalkers passing close by. They heard them talk about a bright, gold world, where the land meets the sea, where the air is hot and dry, and where the sun always seems to be shining.

'Everything is different there,' Rufous whispered to Lantana, 'sandy and sunny.' So they listened carefully to find out how to get to the bright, gold world.

Then the mists came swirling down. The voices faded as the bushwalkers made their way back to the edge of the rainforest.

'Oh Rufous,' sighed Lantana, 'let's visit the land of sea and sand.'

Early next morning, Lantana packed a few things into their bush cart. Then, one behind the other, just like the bushwalkers, Rufous and Lantana made their way to the edge of the rainforest.

Ground pigeons stared from their tufts of grass. Everything looked new and strange.

'I'm not afraid,' said Rufous.
'Neither am I,' said Lantana, close behind.

They rested for a while on a ridge, and sipped water dripping from the rocky ledges.

Then they walked on, around the cliff tops, stopping only to look at the purple orchids high on the boughs of the beech trees.

On and on they travelled, far away from the
rainforest. They passed canefields and cleared
land and farmhouses on stilts.

Lantana ran between rows and rows of
pineapple plants. 'It's a long way to the bright,
gold world,' she said.

On they went again, until a wall of roots
rose out above the mud and barred their way.
The land changed to swampy plains.

Lantana struggled with the cart through the
thick mud.

'Go away biting insects!' cried Rufous. A
swamp kookaburra laughed and flapped its blue
wings. But the crocodile did not stir in the still
waters.

Luckily, the rainforest children found a river.
'This must be the way out of the swamp,'
said Lantana.

So they followed the river, and as night fell they reached the place where the land meets the sea.

Rufous and Lantana were so tired they found safe shelter under the roots of a beach pandanus palm, and they slept through the night.

Next morning, the sunrise warmed their faces and woke them up. They felt the soft sand between their toes. The rainforest children knew they had reached the bright, gold world.

Joyfully, they raced along the beach and
chased the wind-blown grass and tumbled
down the dunes.

In the coral pools they saw sea-stars eat
sand-crabs. But Rufous and Lantana didn't feel
like eating. 'It's too hot,' they both agreed.

They just lazed in the warm blue waters and
watched the sea birds dive.

At low tide they went in search of cowrie shells.
'The sand burns my feet,' said Lantana, as the
sun grew hotter.

Under the sea there were parrot fish and soft
sponges. It was fun hiding in the branching corals.

'But the salty water hurts my mouth,' said Rufous.

'Everything is different here,' the rainforest
children said to each other.

So the days went on. The air was hot and
dry. The sun always seemed to be shining.

It was a bright, gold world.

But after a while, the rainforest children longed to be back behind the curtains of glossy leaves, where they belonged.

'The sand burns my feet,' said Lantana.

'The salty water hurts my mouth,' said Rufous.

'It's too hot for us to eat,' they both agreed.

So the rainforest children left the land of sea and sand, and made their way back to the lush, green world, where the air is as damp as air can be, where tall trees crowd together, and where it always seems to be raining.

Oxford University Press

OXFORD LONDON GLASGOW NEW YORK TORONTO MELBOURNE WELLINGTON NAIROBI DAR ES SALAAM CAPE TOWN
KUALA LUMPUR SINGAPORE HONG KONG TOKYO DELHI BOMBAY CALCUTTA MADRAS KARACHI

Creative direction: Margaret Pittaway

First published 1980

NATIONAL LIBRARY OF AUSTRALIA CATALOGUING IN PUBLICATION DATA

Pittaway, Margaret
The rainforest children.

For children
ISBN 0 19 554238 x

I. Philpott, Heather, illus.
II. Title.

A823'.3

TYPESET IN 14 PT PALATINO BY STL INDUSTRIES PTY LTD, MELBOURNE
PRINTED IN HONG KONG BY LIANG YU PRINTING FACTORY LIMITED
PUBLISHED BY OXFORD UNIVERSITY PRESS, 7 BOWEN CRESCENT, MELBOURNE

Rufous and Lantana's Journey . . .

from the damp rainforest,   through open forest and grassland,